The Three Bears

Illustrated by Elizabeth Webbe

Published by

THE TOON STUDiO

O F   B E V E R L Y   H I L L S

Once upon a time there were Three Bears who lived in a little house in the woods. One of them was a Little Small Wee Bear, one was a Middle-sized Bear, and one was a Great Big Bear.

They each had a bowl for their porridge. The Little
Small Wee Bear had a little tiny bowl, the Middle-sized
bear had a middle-sized bowl, and the Great Big Bear
had a great big bowl.

And they each had a chair to sit in. The Little Small Wee Bear had a little wee chair, the Middle-sized Bear had a middle-sized chair, and the Great Big Bear had a great big chair.

And also they each had a bed to sleep in. The Little
Small Wee Bear had a tiny little bed, the Middle-sized
Bear had a middle-sized bed, and the Great Big Bear
had a great huge bed.

One morning, after they had made the porridge for
their breakfast and poured it into their porridge bowls,
the Three Bears went for a walk in the woods while
their porridge cooled, for they did not want to burn
their mouths by trying to eat it too soon.

While they were walking in the woods, a little girl whose name was Goldilocks came to the house. She looked in at the window and then she peeped in at the keyhole and, seeing nobody in the house, she lifted the latch and went in. There she saw the porridge on the table.

First she tasted the porridge of
the Great Big Bear, and that
was too hot.

Then she tasted the porridge of
the Middle-sized Bear, but that
was too cold.

And then she went to the porridge of the
Little Small Wee Bear and that was neither
too hot nor cold but just right, and she ate it all up.

Next Goldilocks went into the parlor and there she saw the three chairs. First she tried sitting in the chair of the Great Big Bear, but that was too hard. And then she sat down in the chair of the Middle-sized Bear, but that was too soft. But the chair of the Little Small Wee Bear was just right. And she sat in it until the bottom broke.

Then Goldilocks went into the bedchamber where the Three Bears slept. And first she lay down upon the bed of the Great Big Bear, but that was too high at the head for her.

Next she lay down upon the bed of the Middle-sized Bear, but that was too high at the foot for her.

And then she lay down upon the bed of the Little Small Wee Bear, and that was neither too high at the head nor too high at the foot, but just right.
So she covered herself up comfortably and fell fast asleep.

By this time the Three Bears had been walking about for some time in the woods and they thought their porridge would be cool enough now, so they came home to eat their breakfast.

Now Goldilocks had left the spoon of the Great Big Bear standing in his porridge, and he noticed it, first thing.

"SOMEBODY HAS BEEN AT MY PORRIDGE!"
said the Great Big Bear, in his great, rough, gruff voice.
And when the Middle-sized Bear looked at her
porridge, she saw that the spoon was standing in her
porridge, too.
"SOMEBODY HAS BEEN AT MY PORRIDGE!"
said the Middle-sized Bear, in her middle-sized voice.

Then the Little Small Wee Bear looked at his porridge, and there was the spoon in his bowl also, but the porridge was all gone, every bit.

"SOMEBODY HAS BEEN AT MY PORRIDGE, AND HAS EATEN IT ALL UP!" cried the Little Small Wee Bear, in his little, small, wee voice.

Now Goldilocks had not put the hard cushion stright when she rose from the chair of the Great Big Bear, and when he came into the parlor he noticed it, first thing. "SOMEBODY HAS BEEN SITTING IN MY CHAIR!" said the Great Big Bear, in his great rough, gruff voice.

Goldilocks had pushed down the soft cushion in the middle-sized chair

"SOMEBODY HAS BEEN SITTING IN MY CHAIR!" said the Middle-sized Bear, in her middle-sized voice

"SOMEBODY HAS BEEN SITTING IN MY CHAIR AND HAS SAT THE BOTTOM OUT OF IT!" said the little Small Wee Bear, in his little, small, wee voice.

Then the Three Bears thought that they had better search through the rest of the house, so they went into the bedchamber where they slept.

Now Goldilocks had pulled the pillow of the Great Big Bear out of its place, and he noticed it, first thing. "SOMEBODY HAS BEEN LYING IN MY BED!" said the Great Big Bear in his great, rough, gruff voice.

And Goldilocks had pulled the pillow of the Middle-sized Bear out of its place.
"SOMEBODY HAS BEEN LYING IN MY BED!" said the Middle-sized Bear, in her middle-sized voice.

And when the Little Small Wee Bear came to look at his bed, there was the pillow in its right place, and upon the pillow was the golden-haired Goldilocks.
"SOMEBODY HAS BEEN LYING IN MY BED AND HERE SHE IS!" said the Little Small Wee Bear, in his little, small, wee voice.

When Goldilocks heard the little, small, wee voice of the Little Small Wee Bear, it was so sharp and so shrill that it awakened her at once. Upon seeing the Three Bears she ran to the window, and jumped out.

And whether or not Goldilocks ever found her way out of the woods and became a better little girl, no one has ever known. But the Three Bears never saw her again.

The end.